THE MARDI GRAS MYSTERY

LOL Detective Club Book #1

By E.M. FINN

MARDI GRAS MYSTERY: THE LOL DETECTIVE CLUB, BOOK
ONE

Cover Illustration by Steven Bybyk and Natalie Khmelvoska
Cover Design by E.M. Finn

Table of Contents

CHAPTER ONE

"Not again," yelled Lucy Parker as her drink fell off the airplane's tray. Ice water spilled all over her lap, and down into the seat between where her identical twin sister, Lottie, slept. Getting the middle seat on the plane was no fun, but it was her turn this time. Her big brother, Oliver, or Ollie for short, drooled on her shoulder as he slept peacefully in the airplane's window seat.

"Why do I always get stuck in the middle?"

Lucy cried. "Middle child and now middle seat!" The plane hit a pocket of air and lurched, waking both her brother and sister up.

"What's going on? Have we landed yet?" Ollie slurred, still half-asleep. "I had the weirdest dream," he yawned. "I was having a birthday party on an iceberg. A penguin came and jumped on top of me!"

"Yikes! A penguin? Well, maybe it's because of this," Lucy said as she pointed to the ice she had spilled on his lap. "Besides, you just had your birthday party," she snorted.

Ollie had just turned ten years old and he had his very own Ninja themed birthday party. Lottie and Lucy were eight and a half years old. Lucy was three minutes older than her identical twin sister Lottie, which she reminded her of every five minutes.

"Passengers, please prepare for landing," the voice over the intercom said as the overhead call button dinged.

Lottie pushed her dark brown hair out of her eyes as she stretched. "I was having the best dream," she whispered.

"Let me guess," Ollie chuckled. "You were at the library, and they closed for the night. You had to sleep inside with the books."

"Hey, don't make fun of me," Lottie frowned as she playfully slapped Ollie on the knee.

Everyone knew that Lottie loved reading books more than anything. She brought stacks of books with her wherever she went.

"Guys, check out Dad. He looks ridiculous," Lucy laughed as she pointed to the sleeping man in the row across from them.

Mr. Parker, their dad, snored loudly from the next row. He had a photography magazine open across his lap, and his camera bag was stowed at his feet. Mr. Parker worked as a photojournalist for an important magazine. His job was to take photos of some of the most interesting places in the world.

His three children, Ollie, Lucy, and Lottie often traveled with him, and they got to see the best places in the world. It also meant that they spent a lot of time hanging out on planes and trains, traveling to the next exciting location.

This time, they were headed to New Orleans, where their dad was covering the huge Mardi Gras festival. Mardi Gras, also called Carnivale, is a time of celebration when the city of New Orleans puts on a huge party before the fasting of Lent. People come from all around the world to celebrate Mardi Gras in New Orleans. The city comes alive with music and dancing. People dress up in fancy costumes and masks for fun. Best of all is the amazing food of Mardi Gras. Ollie was thinking about the food, especially the donut pastries called beignets, when Lucy interrupted his thoughts.

"I wonder what New Orleans is like," Lucy wondered. "Do you think there will be a mystery for us to solve?"

"There you go with your mysteries again," Ollie laughed. "Why can't we have a normal trip for once, without you turning detective?"

It's true, Lucy loved mysteries and she was always playing the role of detective in the family. She could solve a puzzle faster than anyone. Like the time that their cat stole all of their toothbrushes and nobody could brush their teeth for a week. Yuck!

"Well, you'll be thanking me one day," Lucy said but Ollie didn't hear her. He was pointing out the airplane window at the city below.

"New Orleans, here we come. I can almost smell the beignets," he shouted.

CHAPTER TWO

Their yellow taxicab zoomed into the historic district of New Orleans, called the French Quarter. Horse drawn carriages lined the cobblestone street, and guests were dressed up in fancy costumes for the Mardi Gras celebration. The cab lurched between two horse drawn buggies and dropped Lottie, Ollie, Lucy, and their dad off at the curb outside their hotel.

Lottie looked up at the historic old hotel and let out a gasp. "It looks so spooky!" she cried.

"Oh Lottie," Ollie chuckled. "That's just what hotels looked like in the olden days. This is the historic district of New Orleans."

The kids each rolled their suitcases inside to the wide open courtyard where a serious looking man sat behind the lobby desk. His nametag said his name was Chris P. Bacon, which Ollie thought was a funny name, though he dared not say anything. He held back a laugh as they approached the counter.

"Your name, please?" Mr. Bacon said dryly. He barely looked up from his newspaper as he spoke.

"Oh, Parker Family. It should be under the name Justin Parker," Dad said but nobody could hear him because a dog howled loudly in the background.

"What's that again?" Mr. Bacon asked, his voice rising.

"Parker, Justin Parker," Dad repeated but

the dog howled even louder, making it impossible to hear anything else.

Just then, a soft brown and white King Charles Spaniel leapt from behind the counter and brushed up against Lucy's leg. Lucy squealed with delight.

"I love dogs," Lucy gushed. "I'm crazy about them!"

"Well, you're in luck," Mr. Bacon said. "This hotel, and our sister property across the street, both welcome canine friends. It's so important to be able to travel with your furry family members, don't you think?"

The man's face lit up as he spoke about dogs, and he didn't look so dreary after all.

"I wish we could have brought Daisy," Lucy cried. Daisy was the family Goldendoodle dog that they'd had for as long as they could remember. She was a shaggy white dog that they called Crazy Daisy because she was so wild as a puppy.

"Well, if I'd known they allowed dogs, then maybe we would have brought her," their dad sighed.

"Maybe next time," Mr. Bacon smiled as he watched the kids pet the dog. "While you're here, you're welcome to play with Puddles. She's always hanging around the lobby and she loves to make new friends."

The kids jumped up in excitement. Mr. Bacon smiled and slid his hand under the desk, pulling out a handful of tickets.

"You know, I have a few free tickets to the Mardi Gras showcase happening at the town plaza this afternoon. You should go. It's just a block from here, and it'll be a lot of fun," he said.

"Oh, we couldn't possibly," Dad started to say before Ollie, Lottie, and Lucy all broke into a chorus of, "Please Dad, it'll be fun!"

Dad flipped the tickets over and looked at the back. It said there would be music and carnival acts performing.

"Look Dad, it will be fun," Ollie said. "And it starts in an hour, we have to hurry!"

"Well, alright, we can go," their dad sighed. "I guess you're only at Mardi Gras for the first time once in your life."

The kids ran upstairs to their hotel room and dropped their bags on the bed. Just as they headed out the door, Dad got an important phone call. His face fell as he gathered the kids around the bed for a family meeting.

"Guys, I have a lot of research and work to do to prepare for my photoshoot tomorrow. I'm afraid I can't take you to the showcase in the town square. Since it's only a block away, you kids go and have fun. I'll be here if you need anything. Just stick together and be back before dark," Dad warned them.

"Really, Dad, we can still go?" Ollie said as he jumped up on the bed.

"I'm trusting you. Here is some money in

case you want to buy food or play games. But, be back here no later than sunset, okay?"

Lottie, Ollie, and Lucy all ran for the door, almost forgetting their jackets.

"Thanks, Dad! Bye!" they cheered as the hotel room door closed behind them.

The kids walked down the stairs and out onto the old sidewalk lining the cobblestone street. The sounds of music filled the air, and even though it was mid-day, people were already in brightly colored costumes with masks made of colorful feathers. The air smelled like cinnamon and sugar, and french fries.

As they walked closer to the Festival, they could hear fast-paced Zydeco and Cajun music as people danced in the streets.

"Everything feels so alive," Lottie gasped as she danced in time to the music.

"Don't get too carried away, Lottie," Ollie warned her. "Remember, Dad told us to stick together."

"Do you always have to be such a party pooper?" Lottie teased Ollie, who did his best to ignore her.

Right past the ticket booth, the smell of sweet treats was overwhelming. A food truck was selling king cakes, which are little pastries with a small toy inside. Lottie ate hers right up, but Lucy had one small bite and saved the rest of hers in a napkin for later.

"Let's try the Carnival games next and see if we can win a prize," Lucy squealed. "Dad gave us plenty of money."

"Dad gave us money for food, not games," Ollie said. Then he saw a booth with lots of spy and ninja gadgets as prizes, and his eyes lit up. "Well, maybe it wouldn't hurt to play just one game," he smiled.

Lottie and Lucy tried to throw ping pong balls into fishbowls, and they didn't win anything. But when Ollie tried, his ball bounced right inside the first time.

"You got lucky," Lucy shouted.

"Maybe I did," said Ollie. "Why don't we all pick the prize together? That seems fair."

A set of walkie-talkies hung in the front of the booth, the kind that Ollie had been wanting ever since he saw them at his friend Ben's house last summer.

"I know what you want, the walkie-talkies," Lottie exclaimed.

"Well, they would be pretty cool," Ollie admitted.

Moments later, they all walked down the street trying out their brand new walkie-talkies. Ollie ran up ahead while Lucy and Lottie listened on the other end.

"Paging Mr. Ollie," Lottie laughed.

"This is Ollie, reporting for duty," Ollie barked back, sounding very official.

The girls caught up with Ollie, running past some festival performers wearing brightly colored masks with green and blue feathers.

The performers flew over the street using a trapeze, and scaled the sides of the buildings, flipping off the walls as they danced.

"That's so cool," Ollie shouted. "I wish I had my tablet with me to record this for my blog."

The performers whizzed overhead, jumping and leaping in time to the music. Lucy took another bite of her king cake she had saved in her napkin, and then set it down beside her on a fence post. When she reached to take another bite, her king cake was gone. All that was left were a few crumbs in her crumpled napkin.

"Did one of you take my king cake? Lottie, was it you?" she said, looking accusingly at her twin sister.

"It wasn't me, I swear!" promised Lottie. "Maybe one of the birds ate it when you weren't looking."

Lucy turned her attention back to the street show and watched as one of the masked performers flipped off a balcony and onto the sidewalk beside her. Feathers from his mask fluttered into the street below.

Just then, the kids heard a high pitched scream coming from the direction of their hotel. The scream was so loud, it sounded like it could break glass.

CHAPTER THREE

The kids ran quickly down the cobblestone street, and didn't stop until they slid into the hotel's courtyard.

"We heard a loud scream coming from this direction," Ollie sputtered. "Any idea what's going on?"

Mr. Bacon seemed flustered as a woman with white hair and a long white silk coat sauntered into the room. She wore leopard print high heels and her makeup was thick.

Lottie couldn't tell how old she was, but she looked like a very well preserved great grandma.

"My babies are missing!" she cried out. "Stolen! Taken! Vanished!"

Distraught, she paced the floor before running outside to speak to the police officers who had just arrived on the scene.

"What was that about?" Lucy asked Mr. Bacon, the front desk man.

"Well, from what I can gather, Mrs. Pomador had her usual dog walker take her dogs for a walk today. But when the dog walker stopped at a cafe for a cup of coffee, he tied them up outside. When he came back outside moments later, the dogs were gone."

"Oh no! Did he see who took them?" Ollie asked.

"No, he didn't," Mr. Bacon said, shaken. "And what's worse, I just got a call from the manager at our sister hotel across the street, and two dogs have gone missing over there, as well!"

"That's awful. Tell me exactly what happened," Lucy said as she leaned in closer.

"Oh no, not you and your detective stuff again," Ollie huffed.

"It's worth a shot, Ollie," Lucy said. "It sounds like something strange is going on here at the hotel."

"A similar thing happened with each one," Mr. Bacon continued. "Each time the dogs were stolen when they were outside the hotel. Mrs. Pomador's dogs were stolen when they were out for their daily walk."

"What about the other dogs?" Lottie asked.

"Well, one got lost in the crowd, and the other was stolen from a doggie stroller. At least that's what the manager across the street said," Mr. Bacon explained.

Ollie's eyes lit up. "That does sound suspicious. Any idea who could be doing this?"

"I have no idea. I guess you could say it's a mystery," Mr. Bacon whispered. "I made some flyers for the lost dogs. If you want to help me pass them out, that would be a huge help. I would do it myself, but I haven't got the time because on top of all this, Puddles has gone missing."

"Puddles is missing?" Lucy gasped.

"I'm sure she's just hiding somewhere, Mr. Bacon," Lottie added softly.

Mr. Bacon held back tears as he continued, "She was right here under the desk where she always is, and now I can't find her anywhere. I'm worried she might have been stolen, too," he sobbed.

"Who would have stolen her?" Lottie piped up. "Let's form a search party. She's got to be around here somewhere." Lottie peeked into the huge potted plants in the lobby, and looked behind the couch, but Puddles was nowhere to be found.

"Anything is possible, and anyone could have stolen her. Everything gets so crazy around the time of Mardi Gras," Mr. Bacon sighed. "I'm so sorry guys, I wish I could talk to you all day, but I've got so much to do. Please let me know if you see Puddles," he said as he handed Ollie a big stack of Lost Dog flyers.

The three kids walked to the front of the lobby, away from where Mr. Bacon could hear them.

"There's no way that these dogs have all gone missing like this. There's got to be a pattern," Lucy whispered to Lottie and Ollie.

Ollie shook his head in agreement. "Let's go talk to the police and see what Mrs. Pomador told them. Maybe there's a clue that will help us find Puddles. And maybe we can pass out a few flyers to the police, as well."

The three kids set off down the street, as dusk started to fall over the French Quarter. Crowds of people dressed in brightly colored costumes danced down the street as jazz music filled the night air. The city buzzed with electricity, like everyone was invited to the same big party.

Outside the police station, two officers leaned back against a squad car.

"Hey, that's the officer who was talking to Mrs. Pomador about her dogs at the hotel," Lottie remembered.

"Great," said Ollie. "Okay, you two, let me do the talking since I'm the oldest."

Lottie and Lucy started to protest, but they were close to the police and decided it was best if they looked grown-up.

"Excuse me, Officer Banner," Ollie said, noticing the police officer's name over his badge. "We heard about the missing dogs, and we think someone is stealing pets. We have some flyers here to pass out, as well."

The policeman leaned forward as Ollie spoke. "Well, that is an interesting idea, but why would you think they were being stolen? Lots of dogs go missing during Mardi Gras. It's easy to get lost in a crowd like this," he said as he gestured out to the street filled with party-goers.

"Well, it just seems pretty suspicious, don't you think? Mrs. Pomador's dogs going missing on the same day that three other dogs from the same street went missing," Lucy piped up.

Office Banner thought for a moment. "Yes, that does sound strange. We don't have any evidence to tie these missing dogs together. And besides, why would someone steal a dog during Mardi Gras?" Officer Banner said as he scratched his forehead.

"Well, that's the mystery we're trying to solve," Lucy said confidently.

Just then, Officer Banner's police radio buzzed. "Looks like we've got a situation a few blocks down. Thanks for keeping a lookout, kids. Let me know if you find out anything."

"Well, that didn't give us any leads," Lucy sighed. "We're no closer to solving this mystery than we were before we talked to the police."

Lottie pointed to a sign across the street from the police station. It said, "Barks and Bubbles, The Pet Spa for The Pampered Pooch."

"Let's check this place out before we head back to the hotel," Lottie said. "Maybe she's heard something about the dog nappers, and besides, we can hang some flyers up at her place."

"Great idea," Lucy cheered.

The three kids walked into the squeaky clean pet spa, and were greeted by a small woman with wiry black hair in a neat bun.

"Welcome to Barks and Bubbles. I'm Trudy Doglove, the owner of this establishment," she said. "How can I help, Y'all?" she said in her thick Cajun accent.

"We were wondering if you've heard anything about the dogs that have been stolen today," Lucy said quickly.

"Stolen? Good heavens, no!" Trudy shouted.

"Well, that's just it. We don't know for sure they were stolen. We just heard that some dogs have gone missing. Mrs. Pomador at our hotel, her two rescued greyhounds went missing a few hours ago," Ollie added.

Trudy's eyes lit up. "Those greyhounds were just in here this morning having a bath. I could never forget them, they were so beautiful and sleek. And nervous, too," she said. "Maybe they just ran off. You know how greyhounds can be. They are born to run."

Ollie nodded nervously. He didn't quite know what she meant about greyhounds being born to run. He gave her a stack of flyers and said, "Well, if you hear of anything, please let us know. We're staying at the Dulcett Inn, the same hotel where Mrs. Pomador's staying."

"I'll be sure to keep a lookout," Trudy said as she winked at the kids. "You just never know what's going to happen during Mardi Gras."

CHAPTER FOUR

Lucy flopped on the bed back at the hotel and let out a long sigh. It had started to get dark, and the noise from the street below was loud. It was almost time for bed, but the partying outside made it hard to sleep. Lottie closed the windows and laid down next to Lucy on the bed.

"It just doesn't make any sense," Lucy wondered aloud. "This is a mystery that we need to solve. Everyone else is too busy partying to pay attention to what's going on. And besides, this could help us find poor Puddles."

Ollie was busy playing a game on his tablet, and looked up thoughtfully. "You know, I was thinking, maybe there's something that the police are missing. Something has to tie this all together. It's just that the police have no time to figure it out, since there's so much else going on during Mardi Gras."

"That's what Lucy just said, Ollie," Lottie scolded him. "If you were paying attention and not playing Minecraft on your tablet, you might have heard her."

"Oh, sorry," Ollie said, sheepishly. "And I was not playing Minecraft, for your information. I was updating my blog."

Lucy sat up straight. "This is no time for arguing. I know what we need to do. Tomorrow, let's interview everyone who's had their dog stolen. Maybe we can figure out what links them all together."

"Will that get you to stop crying over Puddles?" Ollie said to Lucy, but he regretted it as soon as he did. A tear slid down Lucy's face and she fell back into the pillow, sobbing.

"Don't worry, Lucy. We'll find Puddles, too," Ollie said as he stashed his tablet on the desk. "Let's get some sleep so we can be ready to interview everybody tomorrow."

The next morning, the sunlight streamed into their hotel room at the crack of dawn. The streets were empty below, and all was quiet and peaceful. At the front desk, Mr. Bacon looked sadder than ever.

"I barely slept. I spent half the night looking for Puddles," he said as he looked up from his newspaper.

"And no luck?" Lucy asked.

"No luck at all," he sighed.

"Well, we're on the case," Lucy assured him.

"Thanks, guys. It really means a lot," he said as his face cheered up a little.

After a quick breakfast in the hotel lobby, the kids walked across the street to the sister hotel where the other pets had been stolen.

Ollie strolled up to the manager's desk and cleared his throat. "We're here to gather some information about the dogs that went missing yesterday," he said.

The manager behind the desk looked suspicious for a moment until Ollie said, "Mr. Bacon sent us over. He said you might know something that could help us find Puddles."

"Oh, of course, he told me you might be coming," the man said. "Let me ring the guests in their rooms and see if they'd agree to meet with you."

After a few moments, the man at the front desk came back and said, "They'll be down in a minute. Just wait right in the lobby."

A curly haired lady bounced into the lobby moments later. In her hand, she clutched a shiny photo of a greyhound dog and a long leash.

She walked right past the kids as she headed towards the front door.

"Wait, ma'am! We just wanted to ask you a few questions about your dog," Lucy shouted after her.

The woman spun around on her heel, and said excitedly, "Oh, Scruffles? We just got a call from the Humane Society saying that he'd been turned in. We're headed that way now."

"That's great news," Lottie said as she hopped to her feet.

"It is fantastic news," the woman said as a wide smile broke across her lips.

"Do you mind if we come with you?" Lucy asked. "Maybe they know something about the other missing dogs."

"Sure thing," the woman smiled. "Just try to keep up," she said as her heels clicked quickly out the door.

The New Orleans Humane Society was just

two blocks down the street and around the corner. The day was overcast and it had started to rain. The kids huddled under their coats as rain pelted up the sidewalk.

The Humane Society was a bright and cheery place, with dogs and cats available for adoption. In the back, several greyhound dogs waited in boarding crates. They looked almost identical, with their sleek gray coats and long pointed noses.

"Scruffles, there you are!" the woman exclaimed. The dog in the furthest pen started whimpering as soon as the woman entered the room.

A volunteer with curly brown hair and soft brown eyes walked in with a clipboard and paperwork. Her nametag said Lupe, and she smiled warmly at the kids.

"You must be Mrs. Dolper," Lupe said as she extended her hand. "I don't know what's going on. It's the weirdest thing. We've had several greyhounds dropped at our front door-step this morning."

"How did you find me?" Mrs. Dolper asked. "We're only in town visiting. I was afraid sweet Scruffles had been lost forever."

"Well, it did take a little detective work. Scruffles has his collar on, thank goodness, and your name is listed. So, we called around the hotels to see if any dogs had been reported missing."

"Oh, thank goodness she was wearing her collar," Mrs. Dolper exclaimed.

"Yes, and she had feathers on her, too," Lupe laughed. "It's the weirdest thing. All the dogs brought in today were greyhounds, and they all had blue and green feathers on their coats."

Lucy and Ollie looked at each other. "A clue!" Lucy whispered.

"Or it could just be that everyone around here wears feathered masks during Mardi

Gras," Ollie replied.

Just then, a young couple walked in the room looking relieved. They ran over to the dog crates and greeted a shy greyhound who had almost fallen asleep.

"Buttercup, there you are," the woman exclaimed with tears in her eyes.

"Well, it looks like this mystery is solved. It's only a matter of time before Mrs. Pomador's dogs wind up here," Ollie whispered to Lucy and Lottie.

"Or is it?" Lucy answered him back. "Why would someone steal these dogs just to return them to the Humane Society? It makes no sense."

The three kids started to walk back to their hotel as the dog owners joyfully reunited with their pups.

"I just know there's more to this," Lucy said. "We've got to put our heads together to figure it out."

"Maybe they were trying to sell the dogs and they got scared," Ollie said.

"Or maybe the dogs really ran away," Lottie offered.

Lucy frowned. "No, the police said that the dogs were stolen. And it's too much of a coincidence that the only dogs brought to the Humane Society today were greyhounds. We've got to get to the bottom of this because I don't think we've seen the last of this dog thief," Lucy said seriously.

By this time, it had started to rain. Droplets fell down on the street and the kids were half soaked by the time they dashed back to the hotel lobby.

Mr. Bacon was asleep at the front desk when they came running inside. He sat straight up when he heard the rumble of their footsteps.

"Oh, I wasn't sleeping. Can I help you?" he mumbled, still half-asleep.

"Mr. Bacon, we didn't mean to disturb you,"

Ollie said sheepishly.

"Oh, it's no bother. I just haven't been sleeping well since Puddles disappeared. I spent the morning posting Lost Dog flyers around the French Quarter," he yawned.

"And she's still nowhere to be found?" Lucy asked hopefully.

"I've looked everywhere," Mr. Bacon sighed.

"You know, Mr. Bacon, we just came back from the Humane Society. They had all the dogs from across the street returned to them today. Maybe Puddles will turn up there."

"Maybe she will," he sighed hopefully. "Or maybe someone will find her and bring her back here. I just got a call that Mrs. Pomador's dogs were found, and the person who found them is on his way over here right now."

"Right now?! He's on his way here right now?!" gasped Lucy.

"Why, yes he is," Mr. Bacon chuckled before the phone rang again. "Excuse me, dear, I need to take this phone call."

Lucy called Ollie and Lottie in for a detective head huddle. That's what she called it when they put all their heads together to think.

Lucy whispered aloud, "This is crazy, you guys! I bet whoever stole the dogs in the first place is the one who is returning them. If we can stake out this guy and figure out why he's returning the dogs, we can crack this case."

"Why do you assume it's a HE anyway," corrected Lottie. "It could be a woman just as easily. And besides, I bet this person who found Mrs. Pomador's dogs is doing a good deed. Don't be so suspicious."

"Let's just see how this plays out," Lucy said. "Follow my lead, okay guys?"

Mr. Bacon hung up the phone and began typing into the hotel computer's keyboard.

"Excuse me, Mr. Bacon. Could you ring Mrs. Pomador and ask if she would meet with us? We would love to hear more about her dogs. I would really love to write a story on my blog about it," Ollie said as he showed Mr. Bacon his tablet with his blog page open.

"I will ask, but Mrs. Pomador's a very private person," Mr. Bacon confided. "Although, she does love good publicity."

Mr. Bacon picked up the phone and dialed Mrs. Pomador's room. After a few "Ahems" and a short explanation, he hung up the phone. "She's agreed to meet with you. You may go up, but let me warn you that Mrs. Pomador is usually very private and very eccentric."

"Eccentric? What does that mean?" whispered Lottie.

"Weird. It means she's weird," answered Ollie.

Mr. Bacon smiled. "Well, I wouldn't go saying that to her face. Her room is on the second floor in the corner. She'll be expecting you."

The kids crept up the staircase feeling full of excitement. The hotel had old carpet lining the halls and red velvet wallpaper. Oil lighted sconces cast an eerie glow down the hallway as they walked towards her room.

At the end of the hallway was a large oak door with a heavy brass knocker. Lucy stood on her tiptoes and knocked three times on the door.

"Here goes nothing," she said as she exhaled loudly.

CHAPTER FIVE

"Come inside, my dears," a musical voice said as the door peeked open. Inside, the room looked unlike any other hotel room the kids had ever seen. The hotel suite was filled with antiques, and it looked like an old European mansion more than a regular hotel room. The windows had heavy red velvet curtains, unlike the plain white drapes in the kids' hotel room.

"Wow! This place is gorgeous," Lottie said as her eyes scanned the walls.

"Oh, yes, I like to make myself at home when I travel. I've been traveling all my life, you see," Mrs. Pomador said sweetly.

She brought out a silver platter of cookies and sugary treats and placed it on the coffee table in front of the sofa.

"Go ahead, sit down," she said. "I hear you have some questions you'd like to ask me for your...what is it? Your blog?"

Ollie studied Mrs. Pomador as she sat down in the chair across from him. She had thin, wrinkled skin and silver white hair. Although she was older than anyone he had ever seen, she was lively and spry. She smiled as she leaned forward towards him.

"I've been staying at this hotel, in this very same room, for seventy years during Mardi Gras," Mrs. Pomador whispered.

"Every year, I get the same room and it's mostly because they let me bring my dogs. I've been a jazz singer all my life, and so I've never had children. My precious pooches are my babies," she confided.

Lucy looked around the room. Mrs. Pomador had framed pictures of the dogs everywhere, even on the nightstand next to the bed. The room looked like a treasure trove of old jazz club nostalgia. In the corner was a large chest, which looked like it might be filled with antiques.

"Mrs. Pomador," Lucy said quietly. "Do you know any reason why someone would want to steal your dogs?"

"Good heavens, no!" she exclaimed. "I'm sure it's all a misunderstanding, anyway. In fact, the gentleman who found sweet Gracie and Greta should be here any moment."

Just then, a loud knock fell on the door to the room. Mrs. Pomador opened the door and two of the prettiest, cleanest dogs the kids had ever seen burst across the carpet and jumped into Mrs. Pomador's lap. They licked her face as she patted their sleek fur coats.

After a moment, Mrs. Pomador stood up and extended her elegant hand to the man who had returned the dogs. Lucy looked closely at the man. She thought she saw a feather peeking out from under his jacket sleeve, but she couldn't be sure. The man was tall and wiry, and his mouth was always moving because he was chewing gum.

"My name's Arthur Kopan," the man said as he shook Mrs. Pomador's hand softly. "I'm so glad I was able to find your dogs and return them to you."

"Let me offer you a reward, my dear sir," Mrs. Pomador said as she reached into her purse. "It's the least I could do."

"Oh, no, I wouldn't dream of it," Mr. Kopan said. "Just doing my duty to spread some Mardi Gras magic."

He smiled through this teeth, but as he spoke, his eyes scanned the room as if he was looking for something.

"Excuse me, Mr. Kopan," Lucy piped up. "We were just wondering how you knew the dog belonged to Mrs. Pomador and how you found her?" Lucy tried not to sound suspicious, but it was hard.

Mr. Kopan looked flustered for a moment, and then said quickly, "Oh, well, the dogs had collars around their necks. I went down to the pet spa to see if someone might know the owner, and she said the dogs had just been in for a bath. She gave me the number for the hotel, and here we are."

Ollie smiled and nudged Lucy with his elbow. "See," he said. "Not everything is a mystery."

Lucy sighed, but something still seemed off about Arthur Kopan. He stretched his arms and walked over to the balcony window. He blew a bubble with his chewing gum as he looked out at the view.

"You wouldn't mind if I got a quick breath of fresh air outside on your balcony, would you? The view of New Orleans is exquisite from this vantage point," he yawned as he stretched his arms wide.

"Help yourself," Mrs. Pomador smiled. She unlocked the sliding glass door of the balcony, and Mr. Kopan walked outside.

Lucy leaned in close to Lottie and Ollie on the couch. They had just about eaten all the cookies and sweets Mrs. Pomador had set out for them.

"Look guys, I know you think I'm crazy, but there's something about this guy I don't trust," Lucy whispered.

Lottie grabbed the last cookie and stuffed it into her mouth. "What do you mean," she said as she chewed with her mouth open.

"Gross, Lottie," Ollie said as he furrowed his eyebrow. "You know, there is something strange about this guy. I know I've seen him somewhere before. I just can't put my finger on it."

As they spoke, Mrs. Pomador's two dogs, Gracie and Greta, came up and licked the crumbs clean.

CHAPTER SIX

Thunder crashed as big droplets of rain fell onto the cobblestone street of the French Quarter. Inside their cozy hotel room, Lottie and Lucy played Minecraft on their tablets while Ollie updated his blog.

"You know, I can't figure out why the dogs were stolen and then returned. It's really bugging me," Lucy said quietly.

"I bet the dogs got loose and ran away. You heard what Officer Banner said. The crowds can get really crazy at Mardi Gras. It would be easy for a dog to get lost," Lottie said. "Or maybe someone out there loves dogs as much as you do and wanted to borrow them for the day," she added.

Suddenly, Ollie jumped up and nearly knocked his tablet onto the floor. "Guys, you're never going to believe this," he said excitedly. "I'm doing research for my blog post about Mrs. Pomador, and look what just came up?"

Lucy put down her tablet and sat down next to Ollie on the bed.

"Two days ago, the New Orleans Tribune published an article about Mrs. Pomador. It says here that she was a big jazz music star in Europe before we were born, and that she performs at Mardi Gras every year."

"We already knew that, Ollie," Lottie said matter-of-factly.

"No wait! Look. It says here that Mrs. Pomador is rumored to own the Inspire Diamond, a rare diamond ring given to her by the Crown Prince of Monaco, among other expensive gems. Then, it says Mrs. Pomador always performs on the final night of Mardi Gras, which is tomorrow night."

Ollie pointed to the picture in the article of Mrs. Pomador, posing with her two greyhound dogs. The caption read: Mrs. Pomador always travels with her prized greyhound dogs, Gracie and Greta.

Lucy jumped up on the bed until she was standing. "I bet the dog nappings and this article are somehow related. What if the dog thief read this article about Mrs. Pomador and then made plans to break into her hotel room to steal her jewelry?"

"But why would they need to steal her dog to steal her jewelry? It makes no sense," Lottie pouted as she went back to her game of Mine-craft. "Besides," she huffed, "Puddles is still missing and I doubt Mr. Bacon has a gazillion dollar diamond ring hiding behind the hotel counter."

"She's got a point," Ollie said as he stretched back across the bed. "Why would Puddles go missing at the same time? And why would the thief steal all those dogs just to get to Mrs. Pomador?"

CHAPTER SEVEN

"Well, I'm going to the police," Lottie said over breakfast. "If something happened to Mrs. Pomador and I didn't warn the police, I could never live with myself."

"You and your mysteries," Ollie laughed.

"No, listen, Ollie. I've had all night to think about it. I think the robber saw the picture of Mrs. Pomador in the newspaper with her dogs, and decided to kidnap them. Then, he figured that he could return the dogs to Mrs. Pomador and steal the diamond ring. Except when he got there, we were there. So, that means he'll be back to steal them later when the room is empty."

"Like maybe tonight when she's singing at the closing of Mardi Gras," Ollie said. "But that doesn't explain the other dogs that were stolen and then dumped at the Humane Society."

"What if the thief stole every greyhound he saw around our hotel, checked their collars, and then returned the ones that didn't belong to Mrs. Pomador?" Lottie said as she munched on her blueberry muffin.

"Excellent point, Lottie," Lucy exclaimed. "Make sure you tell that to the officer when we see him."

Within five minutes, they were down at the police station waiting outside Officer Banner's office.

"What are you going to tell him?" Ollie whispered as Lucy fidgeted nervously. She shrugged her shoulders and began to speak when they heard a voice bellow from Officer Banner's office.

"It's okay, kids, come on in," Officer Banner said as he hung up the phone on his desk.

Before the kids had a chance to sit down, Lucy started explaining her theory to Officer Banner. After she had explained everything, Officer Banner let out a long sigh.

"Well, that does make sense the way you explain it," Officer Banner said. "But, so far, no crime has been committed. All we have are a couple of lost dogs who've been taken to the Humane Society, and two dogs who were returned to their owner."

"But, but, I know something is going to happen to Mrs. Pomador. Please believe me," Lucy begged.

Officer Banner smiled. "The thing is, we can't go around arresting good samaritans who return dogs. Now if she'd been threatened, then we could investigate. Has Mrs. Pomador received any threatening letters or phone calls?"

"No, not that I know of," said Lucy, seriously.

"Well, then I'm afraid I can't help you," Officer Banner said as he stood up from his desk. "Now, if you'll excuse me, I have some official police business to attend to. As you can imagine, we are pretty busy during Mardi Gras."

Lucy slumped down in her chair and frowned. "I know something's not right here," she said.

"Maybe you're right, and maybe you're not," said Lottie. "But there's nothing we can do for now. Let's go back to the hotel and maybe we'll think of something on the way."

The kids walked down the cobblestone street towards the hotel and saw a festival act performing in the square right outside the Police Station. The performers wore feathered masks as they did acrobatic tricks in the air.

"There they are again!" Ollie exclaimed. He

took out his tablet and recorded a video of the acrobatic show. The performers did flips in the air and climbed brightly colored silk scarves dangling from the sky, all while wearing traditional Mardi Gras masks.

"This will be perfect for my blog," Ollie said as he watched the show in awe.

The sky overhead became overcast and the winds grew cold. "Guys, we should go back to the hotel," Lucy said quietly.

"Is it the weather you're hiding from, or do you want to check in on Mrs. Pomador?" Lottie asked.

"Maybe a little of both," Lucy smiled.

"Okay then, I have a plan," Lottie said.

"Tonight, after Dad leaves to go photograph the final night of Mardi Gras, we'll camp outside Mrs. Pomador's hotel room and see if the thief shows up."

Lucy beamed at her twin sister. "Now that sounds like a plan I can get onboard with!" she squealed.

CHAPTER EIGHT

"Come in, Ollie," whispered Lottie. "Ollie, are you there?"

"Yea, I'm here," Ollie said, annoyed. "You're supposed to call me Fierce Ninja, remember? We're using code names!"

Ollie peeked his head out from around the corner. He was holding the walkie-talkie he'd won at the Mardi Gras festival yesterday.

"Oh, right," giggled Lucy. "Fierce Ninja, are you there?"

Ollie turned his walkie-talkie off and walked towards the girls. "If this is going to work, we have to be serious. Let's go over the plan again."

"Good idea," said Lucy. "Lottie and I will be camped in the hallway outside Mrs. Pomador's door. If we hear anything funny, we'll call you on the walkie-talkie."

"But what if Mrs. Pomador sees you and gets suspicious?" Ollie asked.

"Nobody will see us because there's a vending machine in the hallway we can hide behind if we see anybody coming," said Lucy.

"Okay, great. But, where am I stationed again?" asked Ollie.

"You'll be hanging out in the lobby by the front door. If you see or hear anything, you can warn us," Lottie said.

"Sound good?" Lucy said. "Okay, hands together and team cheer on three."

"Team cheer?" Lottie and Ollie said at the same time, both looking confused.

"Oh yes, I figured since we're a detective club and all, we should come up with a team cheer," smiled Lucy.

Ollie and Lottie looked at Lucy, puzzled. "I know I am your identical twin sister, but sometimes I wonder if we're really related," Lottie joked.

"Come on, guys. I thought of a name and everything. We could be the LOL Detective Club," Lucy said excitedly.

"The LOL Detective Club?" Ollie asked as he scratched his head.

"You know, the Lucy Ollie Lottie Detective Club. Put the first letters of our names together and it spells LOL," said Lucy.

"Or the Lottie Ollie Lucy Detective Club," Lottie smirked.

"Right, that works, too," said Lucy. "So, are you in?!"

"We're in," Lottie and Ollie both said as they put their hands together in a circle.

"Go LOL Detective Club!" Lucy chanted.

"Go LOL Detective Club!" they all said together before falling on the floor laughing.

"Alright guys, let's get to our posts. I think we have enough batteries in our walkie-talkies to last a few hours. But, just in case, only use them if you need to," warned Ollie.

"Good point," said Lucy.

The girls snuck upstairs and camped out by the vending machine while Ollie brought his tablet to the lobby and got cozy on a couch by the front door.

"Ollie, I mean, Fierce Ninja, come in," the voice on the other end of the walkie-talkie crackled as soon as Ollie sat down on the couch.

"What is it, Purple Panda?" Ollie whispered into the walkie-talkie. Purple Panda was Lottie's code name.

"It's not Purple Panda," Lucy whispered. "It's me, Crazy Puppy." Lucy's code name was Crazy Puppy because she was crazy about dogs, and even crazier about puppies.

"Make sure you tell us if you see Dad coming, okay?" Lucy whispered.

"Got it, Purple...I mean, Crazy Puppy," Ollie whispered back.

The girls sat down across the hall from the vending machine, and Lucy looked into her pockets.

"I still have ten dollars left from the money Dad gave us for the festival," Lucy said excitedly.

"I'm so hungry," Lottie complained. "We haven't eaten anything for hours."

The girls scooted closer to the vending machine and picked out cookies, candy, and potato chips to eat. Just when they were opening the bag of chips, Ollie's voice crackled across the walkie-talkie.

"Crazy Panda, Purple Puppy, come in," he said in a hurry.

"It's Purple Panda, and Crazy Puppy," Lottie and Lucy shouted at the same time.

"Sorry. It's just that I see Mrs. Pomador coming through the lobby right now. She's getting ready to walk up the stairs!"

Lottie and Lucy grabbed their bags of snacks and hid between the wall and the vending machine. Lottie tried very hard not to giggle as Mrs. Pomador walked by, but she was so nervous she could hardly help herself.

Lucy pinched Lottie in the ribs. "Shhh, we don't want her to see us!" she warned Lottie.

Mrs. Pomador walked by the girls without noticing them at all. She was talking on her cell phone, and clicked down the hall in her tall high heels.

"Oh yes, I took Gracie and Greta to the pet spa to have a massage while I perform tonight. I don't want my dear doggies all alone!" she said. "I'm headed to sing in a little bit. I just need to stop back at my hotel room and get myself ready before the show."

Lottie and Lucy were wedged in very tightly beside the vending machine, and Lucy's leg had started to cramp. Lucy bent her knee to stop the cramp, which hit Lucy right in the leg.

"Oww Eeee!" squealed Lottie, as Lucy covered her mouth quickly.

Mrs. Pomador stopped in her tracks and turned slowly towards the vending machine. She walked up to it but stopped before turning the corner. If she'd walked two inches further, she'd have seen Lottie and Lucy crouched behind the vending machine with their hands over their mouths.

"What was that?" Mrs. Pomador said aloud. "Oh never mind, I think I just heard a dog howling or something," she said to the person she was talking to on her phone.

With that, she walked back towards her hotel room and clicked the lock open. The heavy door slammed shut behind her and the girls let out a sigh of relief.

"Whew, that was close!" Lottie said as she fell into a heap in the hallway.

Lucy crawled out from behind the vending machine sat down next to her sister on the hallway floor. "I'm so glad Mrs. Pomador didn't see us," Lucy sighed.

"And I'm so glad our snacks didn't get crumpled," Lottie laughed as she opened the bag of cookies.

Down in the lobby, Ollie laid back on the couch and pretended to play a video game on his tablet. He was really scanning the lobby, looking for any sign of a suspicious thief. All he could see were tourists and poor Mr. Bacon. He was slumped over the hotel desk, sad about Puddles, who was still missing.

Ollie started to watch the video footage he'd taken earlier that day of the performers at the festival. He clicked to share it to his blog, when he heard a rustle of metal outside the hotel lobby window.

Bang, Clang, Bang. It sounded like someone was climbing the walls of the hotel.

Ollie grabbed his tablet and walkie-talkie, and ran out to the sidewalk in front of the hotel. He looked up and saw a man in black clothes with a feathered mask over his face scaling the balcony of the hotel. Immediately, Ollie saw that the man had climbed onto Mrs. Pomador's balcony. He recognized her balcony by the special red velvet drapes she had hung in her room.

Ollie flipped on the video camera on his tablet and began recording. He yelled into the hotel lobby, "Mr. Bacon, there's an intruder in Mrs. Pomador's room, call the police!"

Mr. Bacon bolted up from his sleep and dialed 911. Just then, a loud scream was heard from upstairs.

"Ollie, Fierce Ninja, come in!" Lucy shouted. "We just heard a scream from Mrs. Pomador's room!"

"I know!" Ollie shouted. "The thief is here. Sit tight and don't let him escape down the hallway."

"You got it," Lucy and Lottie said in unison.

CHAPTER NINE

"I've seen this guy before," Ollie exclaimed over the walkie-talkie. "It's the same guy who was in the Mardi Gras show today doing the acrobatics. I recognize him by his feathered mask."

"You mean, the same feathers they found on the dogs at the Humane Society?" Lucy said hurriedly.

"Yes, the same blue and green ones!" Ollie said as his voice crackled on the walkie-talkie.

Just then, a team of police officers swarmed the hotel. Officer Banner rushed ahead up the staircase towards Mrs. Pomador's room straight past Ollie.

After the officers had passed, Ollie followed them up the stairs to where he found Lottie and Lucy hidden behind the vending machine.

All of a sudden, a giant crack was heard, followed by a loud yelp. The officers kicked down the hotel room door and found the thief laying on the floor with a big diamond ring mark straight on his blackened eye.

"He tried to steal my diamond ring!" Mrs. Pomador shouted. "The one given to me by the Crown Prince of Monaco."

"Calm down, Mrs. Pomador," Officer Banner said as he handcuffed the masked man. "I'm so glad we got here in time."

"In time?!" she said. "I already did all the hard work for you, knocking him out like that with my ring."

"Well, I suppose you did," Officer Banner chuckled. "If it weren't for the call from some young detectives, we might not have gotten here until it was too late."

Ollie, Lottie, and Lucy appeared at the doorway just as Mr. Banner said, "Let's find out the identity of our masked thief. Mrs. Pomador, would you like to remove his mask?"

"Who me?" she said. "Oh Heavens, no. I wouldn't dream of it. Ollie, Lottie, Lucy, why don't you do me the favor of taking off this thief's mask. I do have you to thank, after all."

The kids bent down and lifted the mask off the thief's face. "Just as I suspected," Lucy exclaimed. "It's Arthur Kopan, the dog do-gooder."

"Except he really wasn't doing any good, was he?" Mrs. Pomador said.

"Good work, kids," Officer Banner said as he shook their hands. "We never would have caught this thief without you. You're real Mardi

Gras heroes."

Two police officers carted Arthur Kopan downstairs while Officer Banner stayed behind to make sure Mrs. Pomador was really feeling alright.

CHAPTER TEN

The next morning, after the kids had packed their bags to go home, they decided to sneak out of the hotel after breakfast and make their way down to the police station. They got no further than the front lobby when they saw Officer Banner at the front desk, talking to Mr. Bacon, the hotel manager.

"I'm certainly impressed with you kids," Officer Banner said. "If it hadn't been for you, Arthur Kopan would have stolen the diamond ring and gotten away with it. We questioned him for an hour last night down at the station."

"What did he say?" Lucy asked.

"Well, for one, he planned to steal the diamond on the final night of Mardi Gras, which was last night. He knew Mrs. Pomador would be leaving town today after her show last night."

"But why did he steal her dog and then return him first?" Lottie asked. "He could have just snuck into the hotel room when she wasn't there and stolen the diamond ring."

Officer Banner leaned back against the hotel desk. "Great question, Lucy. Or are you Lottie? Anyway, Mr. Kopan wanted to make sure Mrs. Pomador had the ring in her room, so he wanted to check out the hotel room. And second, when he was up in the room, he asked to go out to the balcony. He put a piece of gum on the lock so it wouldn't latch properly. That allowed him to sneak up and open the balcony door, so

Mrs. Pomador wouldn't expect a thing."

Ollie thought for a moment, and then said, "Except Mrs. Pomador went back to her hotel room to change clothes before the show. I bet he never expected that. He probably wanted to wait for her room to be empty."

"Exactly right," Officer Banner said. "Well, Mrs. Pomador is safe now. And Arthur Kopan won't be stealing any diamond rings again."

"But what about Puddles? Did you find out why Arthur Kopan stole Puddles, Mr. Bacon's dog?" Lucy asked.

Mr. Bacon sat straight up and smiled. "I guess you didn't hear. That's why Officer Banner came in this morning. He found Puddles!"

Lucy jumped up shouting, as Puddles leapt from behind the desk and into her arms.

"There you are, Puddles!" Lucy shouted as Puddles licked her face.

"Puddles is back and not a minute too soon," Mr. Bacon said. "Apparently, she's a bit of a thief herself. She's been eating all the king cakes down at the festival. She waits for people to drop their cakes, and then she grabs them. She's been hiding under the pastry cart, having quite the feast."

"Puddles, I'm surprised you don't weigh a hundred pounds by now," Ollie laughed.

Mr. Parker walked up behind the kids as they laughed, and said, "Well, I guess it's time to check out of the hotel now. We've had a nice, quiet stay at your hotel, Mr. Bacon."

Lottie, Ollie, and Lucy couldn't help but giggle as they rolled their suitcases out of the hotel, and back home to await their next mystery to solve.

The End.

Thank you for reading *The Mardi Gras Mystery: LOL Detective Club, Book One.*

If you enjoyed this book, please leave a review on Amazon! I love hearing what my readers think!

Other Books in the Series:
THE PARIS PUZZLER:
LOL DETECTIVE CLUB BOOK #2

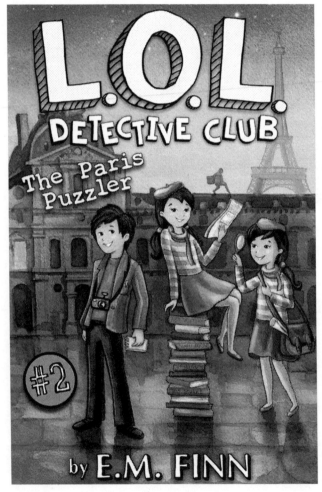

CUBNAPPING IN KENYA:
LOL DETECTIVE CLUB BOOK #3

And more coming soon!

Here is a sneak peek of the next book in the
LOL Detective Club Series:

THE PARIS PUZZLER:
LOL DETECTIVE CLUB BOOK #2

CHAPTER ONE

Lottie Parker fell flat on her face as the train car lurched to a stop. "Paris Metro Station," a voice over the loudspeaker said in a thick French accent.

"That's our stop," her big brother, Oliver, or Ollie for short, shouted as he stood up in the train car aisle.

Ollie was ten years old, and his two younger sisters, Lottie and Lucy, were both eight and a half years old. Lottie and Lucy were identical twins who looked so much alike even their dad got them confused.

"This isn't our train stop, Ollie," Lottie said, as she climbed back into her seat. "We have three more stations to go."

"There's no use arguing. Just ask Dad, he'll know," Lucy said.

Mr. Parker, their dad, was checking his cell phone a few rows down. He had a map of the Paris metro route unfolded on his lap, and his camera bag was stowed neatly at his feet. Mr. Parker worked as a photojournalist for an important magazine. His job was to take photos of some of the most interesting places in the world.

His three children, Ollie, Lucy, and Lottie often traveled with him, and they got to see the best places in the world. It also meant that they spent a lot of time hanging out on planes and trains, traveling to the next exciting location.

This week, they were staying in Paris,

France, where their dad was photographing a special Picasso Exhibit at the Louvre Art Museum in Paris, France. Pablo Picasso was an important artist who lived in the 1900s. He started an art movement called Cubism.

Lottie opened the guide book about Paris she had pulled out of her backpack. "It says here that the Louvre Art Museum is home to the Mona Lisa. You know, the painting of the woman with the mysterious smile," she read aloud.

Lucy leaned in close as Lottie showed her a picture of the painting.

"The Mona Lisa was stolen over a hundred years ago from the museum. Good news, they caught the guy," Lucy said as she read the next page of her book.

"I wonder who stole it?" Ollie mumbled as he played Minecraft on his tablet.

"Well, some people thought Picasso stole it," Lottie said. "But it turned out it was a worker at the museum. It was a mystery for two whole years before they caught him."

"Did you say mystery?" Lucy exclaimed. "You know how much I love detective stuff. Maybe we'll solve our own case while we're at the museum."

"Don't count on it," Lottie said seriously. "It's not like the olden days. The museum has some of the best security in the world. I've heard it's harder to steal a painting there than it is anywhere else in the entire world."

The train lurched forward as it stopped at the next train station. Lottie fell flat on her face, and her bag filled with books skittered across the floor.

"Not again," Lottie huffed.

"I'll help you," Lucy said. She bent down to help her sister pick up her books.

Even though Lucy was only three minutes older than Lottie, they were as different as could be. Lottie loved books and reading. Lucy was crazy about mysteries and being a detective.

As the train car started to leave the station, Lucy yelled down the aisle, "Dad is this our stop?"

"Oh, sorry, I wasn't paying attention. Nope, one more stop to go," said Mr. Parker.

Mr. Parker glanced down at his phone and frowned. "Listen, kids, I've got some bad news. I just got an email that I'm needed across town for a meeting. I'm afraid you guys will have to go to the Museum on your own. I'll meet up with you after lunch."

Lucy's eyes grew wide. Did he mean they'd be spending a whole morning in Paris by themselves, without their dad around?

Mr. Parker handed them three gold passes to hang around their necks. "These badges will get you into the museum for free," he said.

The kids put the passes around their necks, as Mr. Parker handed them each spending money.

"This is for breakfast, and if you need anything else. I want you guys to stick together. And remember, don't touch any of the art. Got it?" Mr. Parker told them.

"Got it," Ollie, Lottie, and Lucy said at the same time.

"Why can't we touch anything?" Lottie asked.

Lucy looked at her sister sideways. "Do you remember that time you touched an eel at the aquarium and you got electrocuted?"

"Your hair stood on end for a week!" Ollie laughed.

"Well, an art museum is just like that," Lucy said. Lottie's eyes grew wide and she couldn't tell if they were joking or not, but she decided not to chance it.

The train car lurched into the next station, and this time, Lottie held on tight. Just as her backpack went flying, she grabbed it out of mid-air. "That was a close one," she whispered.

Mr. Parker jumped out of the train car. As the doors were closing, he said, "Remember to stick together, alright?"

"We will," Ollie and Lucy shouted. Lottie added, "Oui Oui!"

Lucy and Ollie both looked at her funny.

"We we? What does that mean? Do you have to go to the bathroom or something?" Ollie laughed.

Lottie snorted. "No! Oui means yes in French. It's spelled o-u-i, but it's pronounced like we. I've been practicing my French," she said as she pointed to the book in her lap.

"Learn French in Three Days?" Ollie exclaimed. "What day are you on?"

"I'm almost to the end," Lottie said as she snapped the book shut. "You know, speaking French might come in handy. Just wait and see."

Just then, the train dinged as it pulled into the station. "This is it, guys! It's our stop!" Lucy shouted.

Within minutes, Ollie, Lottie, and Lucy walked up to the Louvre Art Museum while Lottie munched on a pastry.

"That looks amazing!" Ollie said as his mouth watered.

"It's called Pain Au Chocolat," Lottie said as she pointed to the phrase in her book. "It's really just a chocolate croissant. But, it sounds better in French. Don't you think?"

"I think it'll sound better when I'm chewing it," Ollie joked.

As they turned the corner, they saw police tape across the entrance to the museum and French police officers asking people questions.

People in the crowd whispered to one another, but it was hard to hear what they were saying.

"We can't understand them because they're speaking French," Lucy said.

"See, I told you that my little book would

come in handy," Lottie smiled.

"Well, don't make us wait. What are they saying?" Ollie begged.

"They're saying that one of the Picasso drawings, worth over a million dollars, has been stolen!" Lottie gasped.

———◆———

About The Author

E.M. Finn writes children's books, including *The LOL Detective Club Mystery Series*.

She lives in Los Angeles, CA with her husband, four daughters, and a goldendoodle named Daisy. Born and raised in Indiana, she moved to California after college and went on to graduate school at USC and UC-Berkeley.

You can find her on her author website, EMFinn.com, and at UrthMama.com, where she has been blogging for a decade about the adventures of raising her four girls. When she's not writing, she homeschools her children and encourages her husband in his film and television career.

Some of her favorite children's books include the *Harry Potter* series, *Nancy Drew Mysteries*, *The Boxcar Children*, and the *Little House on the Prairie* books.

Made in the USA
Lexington, KY
20 May 2019